EMILY'S SURPRISING VOYAGE

SUE PURKISS

EMILY'S SURPRISING ~VOYAGE~

SUE PURKISS

illustrated by
James de la Rue

For my dad, who first introduced me to Mr Brunel's beautiful ship
S.P.

For my Alice
J.D.

This is a work of fiction. Names, characters, places and incidents are either the product of the author's imagination or, if real, used fictitiously.

First published 2010 by Walker Books Ltd
87 Vauxhall Walk, London SE11 5HJ

2 4 6 8 10 9 7 5 3 1

This book has been typeset in StempelSchneidler

Printed in Great Britain by Clays Ltd, St Ives plc

British Library Cataloguing in Publication Data:
a catalogue record for this book is available from the British Library

ISBN 978-1-4063-2182-1

www.walker.co.uk

Contents

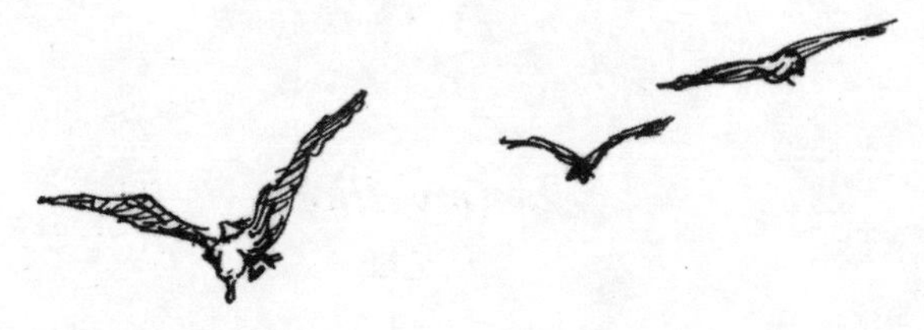

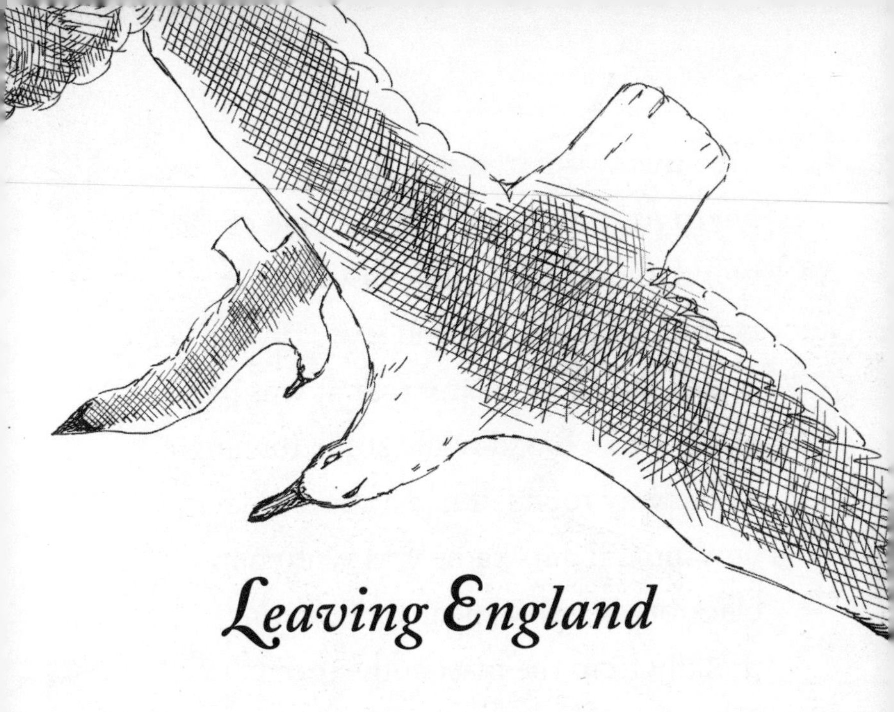

Leaving England

Seagulls screamed overhead and small waves smacked against the quayside. Crowds of passengers chattered and laughed as they waited to board the ship. They were impatient, jostling to get onto the gangway. Emily couldn't understand it; she didn't feel like that at all. The wind tugged at her hat, and she clamped it down firmly on top of her unruly ginger hair as she stared at the curved bulk of the great ship.

So this was it: the ship that was to take her to Australia – to the other side of the world, thousands of miles away from everything she knew and loved. It was very smart, she had to admit that. It was painted black with a broad white stripe running all the way round, it had a shiny golden bowsprit, and its name was written in black on the white pennant fluttering proudly from the mast at the rear: *Great Britain*. A truly remarkable ship, her father had told her – as if that were any consolation!

"Come along, Emily," her mother was saying distractedly. "Do hold my hand – I'm afraid I'll lose you in all this crowd."

"I can't, Mother, I'm holding on to my hat – I don't want it to blow away."

And I'm not going to hold your hand anyway, Emily thought to herself. *I'm not a baby.*

The queue inched slowly forward. Now

they were on the gangway that bridged the gap between the edge of the dock and the ship. Emily glanced down. The sea swirled below, deep and dark and oily. She shivered. What if she fell in? *Don't be silly*, she told herself firmly, *of course I won't. I'd have to climb over the side of the gangway first, and I'm hardly going to do that!*

Emily realized with a start that if she was over water, that meant she wasn't on land any more – that she was no longer in England. She'd been convinced that because she didn't want to go, something would magically stop it happening. But it hadn't, and here she was.

A stupid little tear welled up in the corner of her eye, and she dashed it away impatiently. Then she tilted her head up, set her mouth in a firm line that her grandmother, who knew her very well, would have recognized, and stepped onto the ship.

The captain was there to greet all the passengers as they came on board.

"Captain Gray at your service!" he boomed.

"Henry Ainsworth of Thornton," said Emily's father, bowing. "My wife, and my daughter, Emily."

The captain smiled. He had a kind face, Emily thought, and even though she'd decided to like nothing at all about this voyage, she found herself warming to him. His eyes, deep-set among wrinkles like her grandfather's, were bright blue and twinkly. She smiled back.

"I am truly pleased to make your acquaintance," he said. "Welcome aboard the *SS Great Britain*. She is the biggest ship in the world, and by far the most remarkable."

"Why is that, sir?" asked Emily, looking up at him with interest. "Why is she so remarkable?" Her mother tutted and her father frowned, but the captain smiled happily, clearly delighted to have a chance to talk about his beloved ship.

"Well, for one thing, her hull is made entirely of iron. Think of that, young lady!"

Emily did think about it. "She must be very heavy, then. Why doesn't she sink?"

The captain beamed. "Ha! An excellent question, and one I shall look forward to answering during the voyage."

He glanced behind her. "But in the meantime, I fear that there are other passengers to embark, and the tide to catch, and so our conversation will have to wait."

"Of course, of course," said Emily's father, hustling her on.

"Really, Emily, you must not be so forward!" scolded her mother.

But the captain winked at her, and she did her best to wink back. She hoped he meant what he'd said, and it wasn't just one of those things grown ups came out with. She liked to know how things worked.

She was to share a cabin with Nanny. Nanny's real name was Martha, but everyone called her Nanny because she had looked after both Emily and her mother when they were small. She was the only servant who was coming with them to Australia.

Nanny stood in the doorway, looking round in dismay.

"Oh!" said Emily, surprised. "Is this it? It's quite small, isn't it?"

"Small?" said Nanny, her round pink cheeks puffed out in indignation. "There isn't space to swing a cat! And look at those tiny bunks – they're no more than shelves! How can *I* fit into one of those? I'll – I'll overflow, that's what I'll do!"

Emily's mouth twitched. Nanny was very plump. She was absolutely right – Nanny and that tiny bunk would never work.

But then, *nothing* about this stupid venture was going to work – Emily was quite certain of it, she'd said so all along. Why on earth did her father want to go to Australia? It would take two months just to get there, and for what? As far as she could gather, the place was full of convicts and sheep, and what was the point of *that*? Granny had tried to explain.

"It's to do with business, my poppet. Your father believes it may be cheaper to import wool from Australia for the mill – even perhaps to have a sheep farm of our own – and he wants to go there to look into the possibilities. I know it won't be easy, and I shall miss you terribly. But sometimes the hardest thing is the best."

"Not this time!" Emily had cried. "Not this

time!" And all Granny had been able to do was hug her and stroke her hair away from her face with her cool fingers.

Emily's father appeared at the door of the cabin.

"Ah, Emily, Nanny. Settling in? Good, good, that's the spirit. Cosy, isn't it? Nanny, Mrs Ainsworth needs your help. She is feeling a little faint, I fear."

"As well she might, poor lamb!" said Nanny, casting a reproachful glance at Mr Ainsworth and hurrying off. Like Emily, she believed that going to Australia was a silly idea, and she put the blame firmly on Emily's father.

He frowned and turned to Emily. "I believe the ship is about to cast off, my dear. Would you like to come up on deck? It will be the last we see of England for quite some time."

"I know, Father," she said coldly. And, not waiting for him, she hurried up the stairs.

A band was playing and bright flags fluttered from the rigging. The deck was crowded with passengers calling out last-minute messages to their friends and relatives on the quayside. They were so busy working out whether to laugh or cry that they hardly noticed Emily as she pushed her way through to the ship's side.

The ship's horn boomed out, mournful and deep. Everyone fell silent. It was a solemn moment.

Australia was half a world away: who knew if any of them would ever see England again? Lips trembled, tears trickled down cheeks, handkerchiefs fluttered bravely in farewell. Slowly, slowly, the great ship began to slip away from the dock.

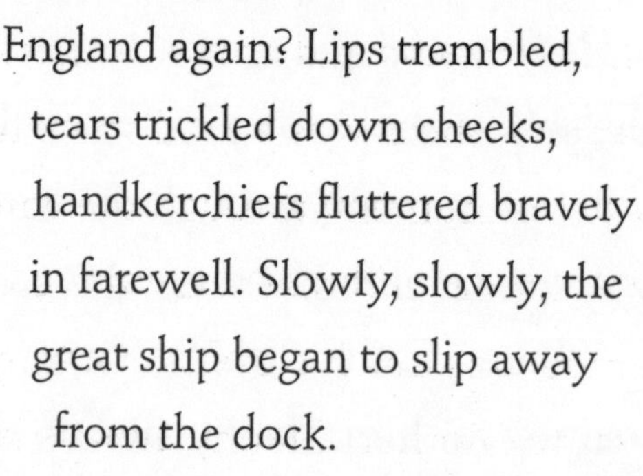

Emily strained to see across the great city of Liverpool, all bustle and chimneys and grime. Somewhere, far beyond, there was an old stone house with a stream running through the garden. That was home, and that was where Granny was. Emily was much closer to Granny than she was to Mother. Granny always had time to play a game or tell a story, or just talk. Right now, she would probably be in the garden, snipping dead heads off the roses or trimming untidy leaves from the yew hedges. Emily could picture her so clearly… The clock on the village church would chime the hour and Granny would look up, and perhaps she would sense that at this very moment Emily was slipping away from her.

Emily's eyes prickled and she rubbed them fiercely.

All of a sudden, she had the feeling that someone was watching her. She looked up, expecting it to be her father. But it wasn't – it was a boy with a thick mop of dark curls.

"I just had something in my eye," she said, wishing to make it quite clear that she hadn't been crying.

He smiled. "Yes. You had an' all."

He had an accent, she noticed, like the people from Thornton, the little town where Grandfather's mill was. She opened her mouth to reply, but before she had a chance, her father was standing beside her, setting his hat straight and looking quite out of sorts.

"Ah, there you are, Emily," he said. "This crowd is dreadful; I entirely lost sight of you. You should have waited for me. And who, pray, is this?"

He looked down his nose at the boy. Emily could see that he was summing up the patched tweed jacket,

the scuffed shoes, the darned trousers, and deciding that this boy was not suitable. Probably not for anything, and certainly not to be talking to Miss Emily Ainsworth, the granddaughter of Sir Richard Ainsworth, the famous mill owner.

"I think you'll find," he said to the boy, "that you should not be in this part of the ship. There's a white line over there, towards the stern of the ship. *Your* place is on the other side. This area is for first-class passengers only. And your cap – you should take it off when you're speaking to a gentleman."

The boy took his hat off obediently. "Yes sir. But I wasn't speaking to a gentleman, sir." He spoke very politely, and for a moment, Emily's father looked uncertain. Then his face darkened.

"*What* did you say?"

"I only meant—"

"Never mind what you *meant*! How dare you be so impudent!"

People were turning to see what was going on, and Emily saw the captain.

"Is there a difficulty, Mr Ainsworth?" he asked.

"Yes, there most certainly is. This young whippersnapper here has just been infernally rude to me!"

"Oh no, sir, I feel sure you're mistaken," said the captain, shaking his head. "I happened to be nearby, and I heard what the young fellow said. I am certain he intended no rudeness. I took his meaning to be that he was talking not to you, sir, but to your daughter."

"What? Well, I—"

Before Emily's father could bluster on, the captain turned to the boy.

"Now then, young man, what's your name?"

"Thomas Drew, sir."

"Well, Thomas Drew, this is my ship. And everyone aboard is under my command, d'you see?"

Thomas Drew nodded, looking a little anxious.

"That being so," the captain went on, resting a hand on the boy's shoulder, "I have an order for you. I would like you to take an important message to one of my crew for me – can you do that? You'll find him in the engine room, down below."

The captain nodded politely to Mr Ainsworth, and just at that moment, Emily noticed something. Something very odd. So odd, in fact, that she could hardly believe her eyes.

For there, poking out between the buttons of Thomas Drew's jacket, was a face. A tiny face, with eyes like black beads and trembling whiskers.

Emily blinked, and when she looked again it had gone. She opened her mouth in astonishment, but before she could say a word, Captain Gray had turned and led the boy away.

Mr Ainsworth looked annoyed. "You must be more careful, my dear," he said abruptly to Emily. "One finds all sorts of riff-raff on board ship. It doesn't do to become familiar with them. Still, you won't see him again. He'll be in steerage, where he belongs. An unpleasant incident, but one which will not, I trust, be repeated."

Emily wasn't listening. She was picturing that little face, with the bead-bright eyes and the long silver whiskers. It was certainly the most interesting thing she'd seen on the ship so far. What exactly was it? She was determined to find out. And that meant she needed to find Thomas Drew again – whether her father liked it or not.

That first evening, however, Emily didn't have a spare minute. First she had to help Nanny unpack. This was no easy task, because the tiny cabin had no room for cupboards, so there was hardly anywhere to put things apart from a few hooks screwed into the wall. In the end, they left most of their clothes in the trunk.

Then they both had to go and fuss round her mother. Her parents' cabin was much bigger. It had a sofa patterned with pink roses, and matching curtains to draw in front of the bunks. Emily thought it was all very pretty, but her mother was unimpressed.

"Why, your father and I can scarcely stand up at the same time," she complained. "It's simply minute. And where am I to put my dresses? Oh, I feel positively faint!" She tried to collapse gracefully onto the bottom bunk, but unfortunately banged her head on the top one.

"Ouch! Henry, this is intolerable – how could you bring me to such a place?" And she began to cry.

Mr Ainsworth backed out hastily and said he would go and look for a steward.

"There, there, madam," soothed Nanny. "We shall manage, Nanny will look after you. Don't I always? Quick, Miss Emily. Get me your mother's smelling salts out of the trunk. Then tip a little lavender water onto a handkerchief. There's nothing a drop of lavender water won't help to sort out."

Eventually some sort of calm was restored, and by then it was time for Emily to have supper with the other children. There didn't seem to be anybody else her age, and she found herself thinking about the boy, Thomas Drew. He would be in steerage, according to her father. Where *was* steerage, and what was it like there? He'd had a very straight way of looking at people, she remembered. She'd liked that.

Later, she lay in her bunk, gazing out of the porthole. A distant light pinpricked the circle of darkness, and she watched it sleepily. On – off, on – off, on – off...

Tomorrow, she promised herself, she would go and look for Thomas Drew and that little bright-eyed creature. Tomorrow…

The Heart of the Ship

When Emily woke the next morning, the *SS Great Britain* was rolling heavily from side to side. It was like being in a rocking chair, she thought, or on a swing in the orchard – up … and down, up … and down. It was really rather pleasant.

But none of the grown-ups seemed to think so. Nanny was groaning in the bottom bunk. Then Father staggered in, looking all white and waxy like a candle. He said Mother was "prostrated", and Nanny must come and help. But when Nanny tried to get up, she was sick, and so he left hurriedly, saying once again he'd find a steward. He seemed to have great faith in the abilities of stewards, Emily thought.

"Is there anything I can do for you?" she asked Nanny helpfully. But Nanny just groaned and flapped her hand feebly, so Emily dressed and set off to find breakfast.

The dining saloon was almost empty this morning; there were just a few small children in the care of their nurses, who looked almost as green as Nanny had. The nurses winced as Emily tucked into eggs and bacon and several slices of fresh bread.

"You're a proper little sailor, you are,

miss!" remarked a steward as he took away her plate.

"Am I?" she said with interest. "Why?"

"Everyone else is seasick," he said. "It's the *Great Britain* Roll. It sorts 'em out every time. Give 'em a few days and they'll get used to it, but in the meantime..." He shook his head and grinned.

"Oh!" said Emily.

So, she was on her own. This was excellent.

"Can you tell me which way it is to steerage, please?" she asked politely.

The steward looked surprised. "Now, why would you be wanting to know that, miss?" he asked.

Emily thought quickly. Clearly, like her father, the steward didn't think that steerage was the kind of place she should go to.

"Oh, I've decided to draw a plan of the ship – for my diary," she said, "and I heard someone mention a place called steerage, so you see, I need to know where it is."

"Oh, that's it, is it?" he said. "Well, miss, it's on the lower decks at the forward end."

"Thank you!" said Emily, heading for the door.

"But you mustn't go there!" he called after her in alarm. "First-class passengers aren't allowed down there, any more than steerage can come up here."

She turned and smiled sweetly at him. "Don't worry," she said. "I wouldn't dream of it."

She closed the door behind her and thought for a moment.

The lower decks at the forward end – that seemed simple enough. She looked round to check that the coast was clear. Then, in no time at all, she was running lightly down the nearest staircase into the hot, noisy heart of the greatest ship in the world.

It was much darker here than on the deck above; daylight didn't filter down this far. With a little thrill of excitement, Emily realized she must be below the surface of the sea.

There was a deep, regular throbbing coming from somewhere below. She looked round uncertainly. Which way now? There were doors on both sides: which to choose? She went over to the one on the right and tugged it open.

Immediately, the throbbing became much louder. There were all sorts of other sounds as well: hisses and whooshes and thumps. That must be the engine room, she thought wisely. Steerage had to be the other way. She shut the door hastily and went over to the one on her left.

Beyond the heavy door was a narrow, dimly lit corridor. There was nothing to show whether this was the right way, and she hesitated. Perhaps she'd got confused. Perhaps you had to go past the engine room to get to the forward end.

Then, just out of the corner of her eye, she saw a pale shape flitting ahead of her along the corridor. She started after it, relieved that there was someone she could ask.

"Hello? Oh..." Her voice trailed off in puzzlement. There was no one there after all – just the flickering shadows cast by the oil lamps. She stared. She *had* seen someone,

or something – she was quite sure of it. Where had they gone? She felt a little annoyed. Whoever it was must have heard her calling. They might have had the decency to answer.

She shrugged and carried on, and soon she could hear sounds: people talking and pots clattering. This was definitely promising. She forgot about the pale figure and pressed on. One more door, and she was there.

It was much more crowded than in first class. The whole of the middle part of the deck was taken up by what looked like bunks, rows and rows of them. Didn't they have cabins of their own down here? There was only a little space round the outside, and that was full of people – some talking and eating breakfast, others looking just as sick and miserable as the passengers in first class.

Everything was very plain, she noticed. Upstairs, the passengers had comfortably padded velvet seats, and ate their rolls and bacon and eggs with silver cutlery from tables covered with white damask cloths. Here, they sat at simple wooden tables and used knives and spoons made of tin.

She hesitated. How was she to find Thomas Drew among all these people?

She walked on uncertainly, expecting someone to challenge her and demand to know what she was doing there. But no one bothered, and she realized they wouldn't

know each other yet, so they wouldn't notice that she wasn't one of them.

Even so, she began to despair. It was so crowded; how was she ever going to find one boy among all these people?

Then, to her relief, she caught sight of his unmistakable mop of dark curls. He was sitting at a table, talking to a woman with a baby on her lap. There, thought Emily, I've done it, I've found him! Feeling pleased with herself, she made her way over to him.

"Hello, Thomas Drew!" she said. "It's me, Emily Ainsworth from Thornton!"

"So it is," he said. "But what are you doing down here? Shouldn't you be back up in first class, where you belong? You know – " his eyes danced – "on the right side of the line?"

She felt her cheeks turning pink. Surely he didn't think she was like her father! But the woman came to her rescue. She looked like Thomas, Emily thought; she had the same dark eyes and curly hair.

"Now, Tom," she said. "That's no way to speak to a young lady. You – oh dear! Oh, my word, I do feel bad! Here, Tom – you take Annie – I must just..." She thrust the baby into Thomas's arms and dashed off, her hand over her mouth, her face the same greenish shade that Nanny's had been.

The baby opened her mouth to cry, and Thomas passed her over to a startled Emily.

"Here," he said. "You sit down with her and I'll give her some porridge. She's hungry, that's all."

Emily didn't know any babies, so she had no idea what to do with this one. Annie felt warm and slightly damp, and Emily held her awkwardly at arm's length.

"Not like that! Haven't you ever held a baby before? Here – you have the spoon and I'll have Annie."

He settled the baby comfortably against his chest and nodded at Emily, who nervously offered her a spoonful of porridge.

"Taste it first," ordered Thomas. "You have to make sure it's not too hot. Honestly – don't you know *anything*?"

The porridge was warm and sweet. Emily quite liked it and so did Annie, who ate it happily and opened her mouth for more.

"Yum, yum!" said Thomas, jiggling Annie gently up and down. "That's lovely, isn't it? Lucky Annie! So," he said then, looking at Emily curiously, "what *are* you doing here?"

"Yesterday," said Emily, offering Annie another spoonful, "when my father was talking to the captain, I noticed something inside your jacket. They didn't see, but I did. You've got a pet, haven't you? You brought an animal on board, and I'd like to know what it is."

"Don't know what you're talking about," said Thomas cheerfully. "You must have been seeing things."

"Yes," said Emily, pointing with the spoon. "And I'm seeing them again now!"

And there it was. The tiny face, with black beady eyes and busily twitching whiskers.

"Oh!" said Emily, her eyes widening as she suddenly realized what it was. "It's a *rat*!"

Then several things happened at once. The door to steerage was flung open and the captain's voice boomed out. Thomas jumped up and Annie bawled in protest. Mrs Drew reappeared, looking shaky and pale. She took Annie from Thomas and shushed her. Thomas threw an urgent look at Emily and put a finger to his lips, and everyone turned to stare at the captain.

"Now, ladies and gentlemen of the steerage! Those of you who are upright, seize a brush and a bucket and set to! You must keep your quarters clean, everything must be kept shipshape and Bristol fashion. Mr Rigby here will show you where everything's kept. And then, I want everyone who can walk to go up on deck. Fresh air, that's the ticket – that's what'll keep you all healthy!"

Then he caught sight of Thomas and Emily and raised his eyebrows in surprise.

"Ah! We met yesterday, didn't we? Now, let me think – I have an excellent memory for names. Drew, wasn't it? Master Thomas Drew. And – Emma? No, wait, I have it – Emily! Hmm … yes, you were with your father. And you were interested in my ship. And this is your mother, is it, Master Drew? And a little sister – or perhaps a brother?"

"A sister, sir," said Mrs Drew proudly. "I have four children, sir, and every one a treasure."

The captain nodded. "I've no doubt of it, madam," he said. "I'm sure they do you proud. And Thomas is the eldest?"

She nodded. "Yes, sir. In between there are Meg and Jack. They and their father are sick as dogs at the moment, and I'm not much better."

"It will pass," he said, "it will pass. Well,

take care. Rest and fresh air, madam – that's my prescription!"

He smiled and strode off, his hands clasped behind his back, looking from side to side, encouraging and barking at people in turns.

"There," said Mrs Drew to Thomas. "You heard what the captain said. Go up on deck for a while." She glanced at Emily. "With your friend."

He looked undecided. "But what about you, Mam? And Annie?"

"She's ready for a sleep, bless her, and so am I. Don't you worry about us. Off you go!"

As they went back along the dark corridor that led from steerage, Emily remembered the pale figure she'd half glimpsed. She hesitated and glanced round curiously.

"When I came along here just now," she said, "I thought I saw someone. It was only for a second, and then they just seemed to disappear."

"Perhaps it was a ghost," said Thomas. "The ghost of a drowned sailor!"

"I never thought of that! Perhaps it was." Emily felt a little thrill of fear.

He grinned. "We'll watch out for it! Anyway, come on."

She followed. But she kept close to Thomas until they were out in the daylight again.

Up on deck, Emily drew in a deep breath of fresh air. Then she turned eagerly to Thomas. "Please let me see the rat," she said. "What's it called? Does it bite?"

"Shh!" he said, looking round anxiously.

"This is a ship. It's *full* of rats. If anyone sees Barney, they'll think he's just an ordinary rat, and they might – well, they would – *kill* him. And I've had him since he was a baby, and I couldn't bear that."

"I won't tell," promised Emily. "Honestly, I won't. But please let me see him!"

Thomas looked at her seriously. "What do you care about most in the world?" he said.

She thought. "It's not a what, it's a who. It's my grandmother."

"Right. Well, you must swear on your grandmother's head that you won't tell anyone about Barney. And then if you do tell, something really awful will happen to her, because you'll have broken your solemnest word."

Emily's eyes opened wide. "That's terrible," she said. "I won't do it!"

"Suit yourself. But if you don't, I won't show you Barney."

She hesitated. But she couldn't just walk away. And she never told tales anyway. "All right," she said reluctantly.

"Say it. Swear it."

She sighed and rolled her eyes. "I swear on my grandmother's head that I won't tell anybody about Barney."

He nodded, satisfied, then glanced round cautiously. Some sailors were working at the other end of the ship, and a few passengers were strolling round or gazing out to sea, but there was no one close by. Thomas

undid the top buttons of his waistcoat and carefully drew out a leather pouch which had been hanging on a drawstring round his neck. The neck was loose, but he eased it open further – and out onto his outstretched hand popped the little face, followed by a small brown body and a long black tail.

Emily stared, fascinated, as Thomas tickled the little creature's throat. It rubbed its head against his hand, and licked it enthusiastically.

"But won't he run away?"

He shook his head. "We're close, me and Barney. Like I said, I've had him since he was a baby. I used to work on a farm, see,

and one morning I was in the barn – that's why he's called Barney – and I saw one of the cats playing with something. I think it was Barney's mum. Well, she was already dead, but then I heard this squeaking."

"Barney?" guessed Emily.

Thomas nodded gravely. "But not just Barney. There were six of 'em, all curled up in a nest in the hay. But before I could get to 'em the cat pounced, and that was that. Barney was the only one I could save. I've looked after him ever since, but then Mam said I had to set him free, because he wouldn't be allowed on board the ship, and I pretended to, but I didn't. I made the bag and I've kept him hid. But I don't know how much longer I can keep him safe. You've seen how crowded it is in steerage. Someone's bound to see him sooner or later, and *then* there'll be trouble!"

"Does he bite?"

"'Course he doesn't, he's as tame as

anything. He's a little charmer, is Barney."

"Can I stroke him then?"

Thomas held out his hand and she drew a finger along Barney's back. The fur wasn't soft like a cat's, but it was smooth and gleaming. Barney closed his eyes and stretched out happily.

"He likes me!" she said in delight. "Look – you can see that he does!"

"Yes," agreed Thomas, "he does."

"Oh, look! He's sitting up, just like a little person!" said Emily. "Look at his paws, they're like tiny hands."

Thomas was looking at her, considering. "Do you have a cabin, Emily?"

"Yes, of course," she said. "Why?"

He didn't say anything at first, and she glanced at him. His eyes were dark, with very long eyelashes. She wished she had dark eyes and black curls instead of frizzy ginger hair and wishy-washy green eyes.

"Because I was just wondering... Oh no, it's not fair. If anybody found him you'd be in trouble. No, forget it – it was a silly idea."

"What was? What are you talking about?" Then, "Oh! You want *me* to look after him! But it's not just my cabin, Nanny sleeps there too."

"Nanny! Aren't you a bit old for a nanny?"

She bristled. "That's just what she's called. She looks after Mother, not me. *Do* you want me to look after Barney, or not?"

"What would you keep him in?" said Thomas doubtfully, just as if it hadn't been his idea in the first place.

"*I* don't know," she said, exasperated. "Where does he usually sleep?"

"Well, last night he had to sleep next to me in his pouch. But at home he had a box with straw in it."

Thinking fast, Emily said, "I've got a hatbox! I could tear up the tissue paper – it would be almost as good as straw. And I could make holes in the lid to let the air in. What does he eat?"

"Oh, all sorts. He likes oats and bread, bits of apple, cheese – almost anything." His eyes shone. "Do you really think you can do it? Won't this Nanny person notice?"

"Not at the moment," said Emily, "she's far too sick. When she's better, we might have to think of something else. But till then, Barney will be safe with me."

Thomas held Barney up to his face. "Do you hear that, Barney? You're going to be safe! Me and Emily are going to take care of you, aren't we, Em?"

She smiled in delight. She'd found a friend, and she'd found a pet. She felt happier than she had for weeks.

"Yes, Tom, we are!"

Looking After Barney

For several days, everything went exactly as planned. Barney seemed delighted with his hatbox home, and Emily spent hours playing with him and feeding him. Nanny had got over her seasickness much more quickly than Mother and Father had, but she bustled off to look after them anyway, and so Emily and Barney had the cabin to themselves. At least once a day she tucked him into his pouch and went off to meet Tom, and together they explored the ship. Her parents probably thought she was reading, or writing in her journal, if they thought about her at all. She didn't think they really minded much, so long as she wasn't under their feet. Sometimes they bumped into Captain Gray as he went on his rounds, and he told them stories about his beloved ship.

"She was designed by Isambard Kingdom Brunel," he said. "It's a fine name, isn't it? A fine name for a fine man – and a fine engineer. When she was launched, fireworks lit up the sky all over Bristol. Mr Brunel's big ship, they called her. Everyone came to watch her go – the first ship with a steel hull, and the biggest to be driven by steam."

"Steam?" said Emily. "Like trains?"

"Yes, young Emily. Exactly like trains. But on a train, the pistons drive the wheels. On the *Great Britain*, they drive the propeller – and that's what pushes her through the water. Though she does have sails as well, so she can catch the wind. That saves on fuel, d'you see? And that's good, because she can carry only so much coal."

He took them down to see the engine room. It throbbed like a giant metal heart, and the heat was unbelievable. The steam to drive the pistons was created by coal fires which heated a massive boiler. Emily didn't envy the stokers whose job it was to feed the greedy fires, shovelling coal constantly in four-hour shifts.

Their eyes glittered through faces black with soot, and their powerful arms moved in tune with the engine, just as if they were part of it.

"If it wasn't for them, the ship wouldn't go, would it?" she said later to Tom, watching him as he played with Barney in an empty cabin they'd discovered. "It must be a horrible job. I wouldn't like it."

"No, I don't suppose you would," he said, glancing at her. "And I don't suppose you'd like working in your grandfather's mill, either."

"Why do you say that?" she asked, surprised. "What do you know about Grandfather's mill?"

He looked at her steadily. "Plenty. It's the Ainsworth Mill, isn't it? In Thornton. I realized who you were when you said your name and where you come from. My father worked in it, and so did I. Meg and Jack would have gone there too if we'd stayed.

But Father said it was bad enough *his* lungs being all clogged up – he wouldn't stand for it to happen to all of us." His eyes shone. "That's why we're going to Australia. We'll have our own farm there. They've got lots of land, and they need people to work it. It'll be hard, but it won't matter, because we'll be working for ourselves and not for some greedy mill owner."

"Grandfather isn't greedy! And I'm sure his mill can't be a bad place to work," she said hotly. "He looks after his workers, I've heard him say so. They're very important to him."

Tom smiled. It was a funny sort of smile, and she didn't like it. "Have you ever been inside the mill?" he asked.

She shook her head unwillingly.

"No, of course you haven't. The noise from the machines – it's terrible, you can't hear yourself think. And you can hardly see. It's like a thick white mist with lots of tiny bits of wool floating about, clogging up the air, getting up your nose, tickling your throat. Father coughs all the time, but he can't get rid of them. Funny way to look after people."

"Well, Grandfather can't know about that," she said, dismayed. "He's a kind person. I'll tell him, and he'll do something about it, I know he will."

But she couldn't tell him about it, she realized. She might never see him again.

"I'll write to him," she burst out. "I will, I promise!"

Tom took a marble out of his pocket and rolled it for Barney. He watched the little rat scamper after it and clutch it between his paws. "It won't make any difference. The mill will still be there. People will still get sick, and be injured by the machines."

She glared at him and stood up. How dare he say such things? Her grandfather wouldn't purposely do anything to hurt anyone, she knew he wouldn't.

"I'm going back now," she said. "Give me Barney and I'll put him in his box. A lady called Mrs Pettigrew is starting a school for the little children, and she asked if I would help her in the mornings. I won't have time to come down and see you any more."

"You're not the only one who's going to be busy," snapped Tom. "The captain says I can work in the bakery. I'll get paid, and I'll get fresh bread for us too. I won't have time to waste either."

"I'll look after Barney by myself then," she said, "if that's what you want."

Tom was still for a moment. Then, without looking at her, he said, "I wish I could have him with me, but he wouldn't be safe.

You – you *will* take care of him, won't you?"

"Of course," she said stiffly, though she was determined not to forgive him for the things he had said.

He carefully handed Barney to her. Then he turned round, and walked off without looking back.

That had been two days ago, and Emily hadn't seen Tom since. She hated that they'd fallen out, but he'd been horrid about her grandfather, and she wasn't going to be the one to make up. She thought a lot about what Thomas had said about the mill. How could it be true? But then again, what reason would he have to lie? She tried to ask Nanny about it, but she wasn't much help.

"What's it like in the mill?" Nanny repeated. "Why, how in the world should I know? It's not my place to know about the mill, nor yours either. Whatever made you think of such a thing? That's your grandfather's business, and your father's, and I'm sure everything's just as it should be. Now, I must get on. Your poor mother, she's still not feeling well..."

And with that, for the time being, Emily had to be content.

She lay on her bunk, watching Barney eating a piece of apple. He was sitting on his haunches in his hatbox house, holding the apple in his paws, nibbling it daintily. After he'd finished, he carefully licked himself clean, and then looked seriously at Emily.

"You want some more, don't you?" she said. "I think you like apple. I think it's your favourite thing, except for bacon rinds. They're the best, aren't they? I'll get you some more tomorrow, if—"

"Come along, Miss Emily! Whatever are you doing, idling around in here? And whoever were you talking to? Your mother is feeling much better today, and she wants to see you."

Emily froze. She'd thought Nanny was safely out of the way.

"Miss Emily? Come along now, let me see if you've washed behind your ears. What's that you've got up there? Your hatbox? What's that doing on your bed?"

Usually the box was beside the wall and out of sight from below. Emily had been careless – very careless. She scooped Barney up, pushed him into the pouch that hung round her neck inside her pinafore, and rammed the lid onto the hatbox. Then she dangled her legs over the side of the bunk, ready to jump down.

"I've been using it to keep things handy," she

said innocently. "My book and my diary and my drawing things."

"Oh yes? That's nice, dear. Now, where's that piece of ribbon – you know your mother likes you to look nice." Emily put up with having her hair brushed till it hurt and tied back neatly. It was all a waste of time, she thought to herself. No matter what Nanny did, Emily would never be pretty enough for her mother.

Mrs Drew was draped elegantly on a sofa in the ladies' sitting-room, fanning herself gently as she talked to two of her friends.

"Ah, here she is! Lady Russell, Mrs Mortmain; may I present my daughter, Emily?" Emily dropped a little curtsey. The ladies cooed and her mother looked pleased.

"Are you feeling better, Mother?" she asked politely.

"A little, my dear, a little. I fear that life at sea has not agreed with me so far.

But Mrs Mortmain here has been kind enough to tell me all the news. It seems that now we are all emerging from our afflictions, there will be much to entertain us, so I am feeling greatly cheered."

"Oh?" said Emily.

"Yes indeed," said Mrs Mortmain, a small, bird-like lady with bright dark eyes and a sharp chin. "There are to be dances, theatricals, concerts – all manner of things! But, my dear, I have not told you the most exciting news of all!" She raised her lorgnette and gazed at the others triumphantly. "There is a *ghost* on board!" Lady Russell raised her eyebrows,

Mrs Ainsworth gasped, and Emily leaned forward. Now this really *was* interesting!

"A ghost?" she asked. "Are you sure? What does it look like?"

"A pale figure, in the shape of a boy. It is perfectly true. Our steward told me all about it. He *almost* saw it himself – a mysterious light, flickering at the end of the corridor that leads to the pantry. Several people have seen it, flitting and fluttering about in – in a ghostly kind of a way. And..." She paused impressively.

"Yes?" said Lady Russell breathlessly.

"And only yesterday, Colonel Digby was obliged to get up in the night, to... I don't quite know why, but anyway, he saw a pale figure, and when it saw the colonel, it let out the most bloodcurdling shriek. Mrs Digby assured me the colonel's hair was several shades whiter in the morning, she was quite certain of it!"

"*Really*?" said Mrs Ainsworth. "But this is dreadful! To be trapped on a ship with a ghost... Oh, my goodness, I begin to feel quite faint again! Emily, my smelling salts, they are in my reticule – please – quickly!"

Hastily, Emily fumbled in Mrs Ainsworth's bag for the smelling salts.

Suddenly she heard a scream. It was the loudest, shrillest, most piercing scream Emily had ever heard. She'd had no idea her mother could scream like that.

Then, clutching her skirts, her mother leapt off the sofa. Lady Russell and Mrs Mortmain stared in astonishment. Alerted by the scream, a steward shot through the door.

He was followed by the barber, who had set up shop in a nearby cabin, then by his customers, then by sundry other passengers who happened to be passing.

Soon the small room was crammed with people, all transfixed by the sight of Mrs Ainsworth pointing a trembling finger at Emily. She was trying to speak, but her face was fixed in a rictus of horror. Finally, she managed to croak out a whisper.

"There was a face! The face of – of a *rat*! Right there, peering out at me, from just underneath Emily's chin!"

They all turned to gape at Emily, but then her mother rolled her eyes, clasped her hand to her forehead, and fainted in the most dramatic manner possible. Everyone clustered round her, and Emily seized her chance. She slipped out of the sitting-room, ran through the dining-room, and hurtled down the stairs in search of Tom.

She almost crashed into him as he came out of the bakery with a tray full of rolls balanced at shoulder height.

"You idiot!" he hissed. "Are you trying to get me the sack?"

"No, of course not," Emily said indignantly. "I came to find you, and I think you might be a little more grateful. It's Barney – he's in danger!"

"Why? What's happened? Is he all right?"

"Yes," said Emily, patting the pouch. "He's here. He's fine, but only for now. He's not safe with me any longer." And she explained what had happened.

"You let your mother see him?" he said in disbelief. "How *could* you be so stupid?"

How *could* he be so unfair?

"No stupider than you were," she said indignantly. "I saw him twice when you were looking after him, remember? Anyway, this isn't helping. The important thing is, I can't keep him with me any longer, and you can't keep him with you – so what are we going to *do*?"

"Find somewhere else. Somewhere safe. Somewhere people don't go." He thought for a minute, then he brightened. "I know! The hold! No one ever goes down there, and anyway I bet there's lots of good hiding places. You can fetch his box, and we can go and see him and take his food down. He'll be right as ninepence."

"The hold?"

"Yes, where they keep the cargo. Don't you remember? Captain Gray showed us

where it was when we went on his rounds with him. He said that the *Great Britain* carried soldiers once, and the officers kept their horses down there."

She nodded slowly, picturing it. She hadn't liked the hold much. It had been dark, and full of strange creaks and groans. "Yes, I remember it. But how do I get there?"

"There's a staircase at the end of the first-class cabins. Get the box, go all the way down, and I'll meet you at the entrance as soon as I can."

It was almost completely dark in the hold; the occasional dim lantern fixed to the walls only served to throw up huge looming shadows. Emily looked round nervously, and stuck very close to Tom. Something soft and clinging touched the back of her neck; she squeaked in fear, but then realized it was just a cobweb.

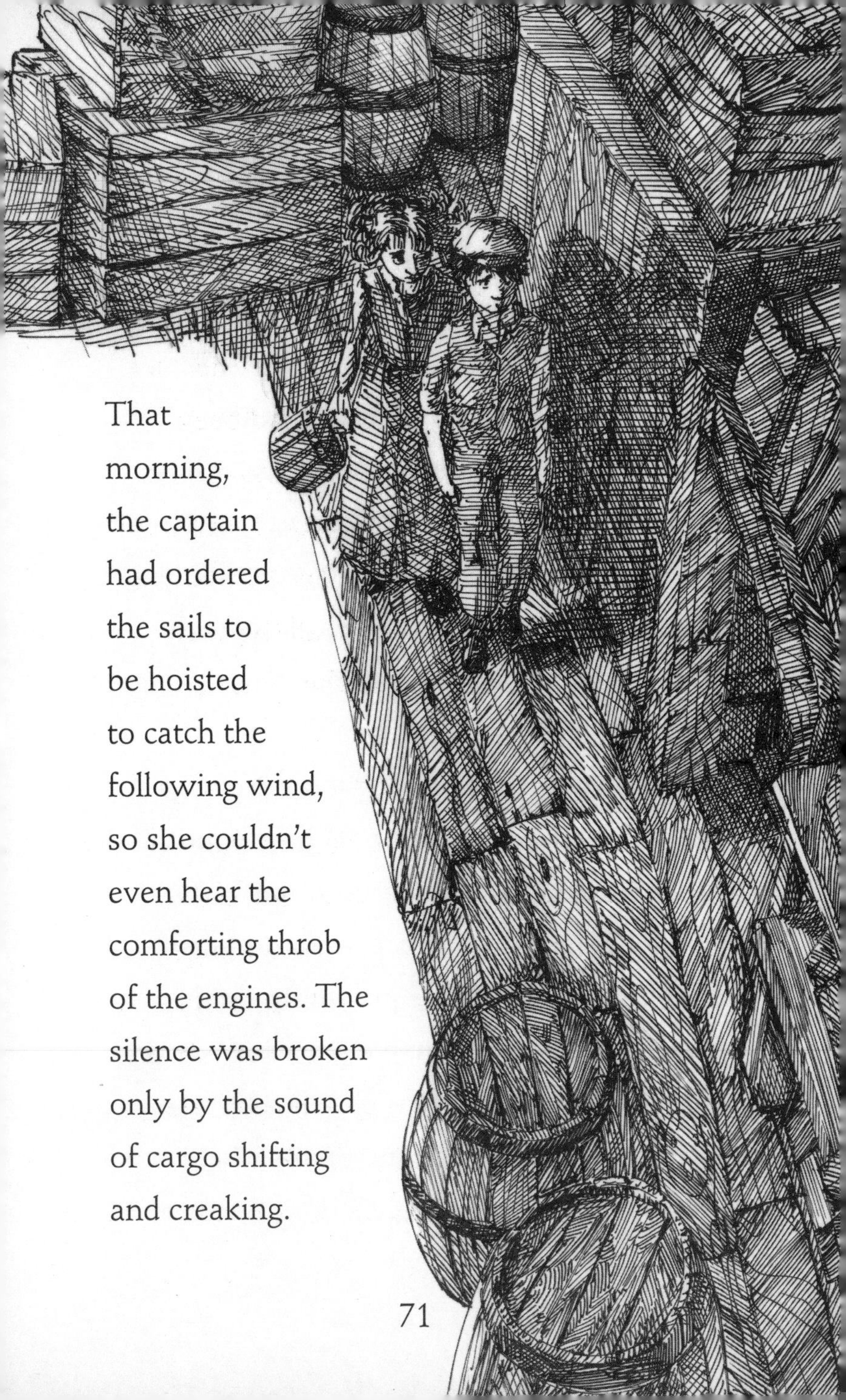

That
morning,
the captain
had ordered
the sails to
be hoisted
to catch the
following wind,
so she couldn't
even hear the
comforting throb
of the engines. The
silence was broken
only by the sound
of cargo shifting
and creaking.

Then she heard something else: squeaks, and a skittering, scurrying sound. Emily gulped. She knew what the sound was, Captain Gray had told them. It was the ship's rats. She loved Barney, but she didn't feel at all the same about these other, nameless rats. According to Captain Gray, some of them were little short of monsters.

"Why, they're as big as cats, some of 'em," he'd declared. "They've teeth as sharp as scissors. You don't want to meet a ship's rat on a dark night, I'll tell you!"

"Do you think Barney will be safe down here?" she said nervously. "What about the other rats? They might attack him."

"We haven't any choice, as far as I can see," said Tom. "We've just got to do the best we can. Come on, we'll put his box on top of this cask – he'll be as safe as houses." He put the box down, and then paused. "Hold on a minute – what's that? Look, over there – a light! Somebody's down here. Shush!"

"Why would anyone else have come to the hold?" whispered Emily.

"I don't know," Tom whispered back. "The captain said that there's no reason for anyone to come here during the voyage. It just has the cargo that's being taken to Australia."

Emily felt uneasy as she watched the dim, flickering light. "It's not a person," she murmured. "We'd be able to see him. A person would be taller than those packing cases." Then she gasped. "I know what it is – it's the ghost, it must be!"

"Ghost? What ghost?" he said, so surprised he forgot to whisper.

"The ghost that's haunting the ship," she said fearfully. "Mother's friend was telling us – lots of people have seen it. I think it must have been what I saw when I came down to steerage. I told you about it, don't you remember? It was pale, and it disappeared into thin air, it really did!"

The light began to bob up and down, weaving slowly towards them. It made the darkness seem even darker. Anything could have been hidden in that darkness, anything at all. Emily's heart thudded against her chest, and when she at last found her voice, it was no more than a terrified squeak.

"It's coming to get us!"

"Quick – back towards the stairs!"

Out of the hold and with the door safely slammed shut, they stopped to catch their breath.

"Did you see what it was?" panted Emily. "Properly, I mean?"

"No. Just the light."

They both thought about a pale mysterious light that moved all by itself. Then Emily took a deep breath.

"We can't leave Barney in there. It's not safe. Not with all those huge wild rats and – and a ghost!"

"I know," said Tom. "I was just thinking the same. We've got to go back in. We've got to fetch him. Ready?"

She nodded, and he gave her an encouraging smile.

"Come on then, quiet as you can."

Emily wasn't sure that being quiet would make any difference to a ghost, but she didn't want to think about that: all she knew was that if she didn't go back into the hold straight away, she never would.

So the two of them crept back into the dark heart of the ship, determined to rescue Barney.

The Secret of the Hold

At first everything was as black as night. But gradually their eyes adjusted, and once again they saw the dim bulk of barrels and packing cases.

"Past these two barrels," counted Tom, "round the corner, and – ouch!"

"What?" gasped Emily.

"Nothing. I just stubbed my toe. Now, left down here..."

"It's there," breathed Emily. "The light.

It – it's right beside Barney's box."

They stopped and looked at each other.

"Ready?" whispered Tom. "We creep up very quietly, we grab the box, and we run. Do you want to hold my hand?"

"Yes," whispered Emily, "I do." She would have held anybody's hand, as long as there was a real live person on the other end of it.

Emily trembled as they crept closer. What would they see when they reached that mysterious flickering light? She imagined a drowned sailor trailing seaweed, bones picked dry by fish, a crab crawling out of an empty eye socket... For two pins, she would have turned round and fled, but they had to rescue Barney. And then she saw the ghost and stopped short in astonishment.

It wasn't a ghost, though it did look like one. It was a boy: bone thin and white as chalk, with great circles under his eyes, hollow cheeks, and dirty rags for clothes.

He had put the stub of a candle on the shelf beside Barney's hatbox, and in its flickering light they saw that he was holding Barney, gazing at him so intently that he didn't notice Emily and Tom.

"Got you!" cried Tom triumphantly.

The boy clutched Barney to himself with one hand. He threw the other arm in front of his face, and shrank back, terrified.

"Oh, Tom, don't be such an idiot! He's only little, and he thinks you're going to hit him." And instinctively, Emily reached out and said softly, "It's all right. We won't hurt you, I promise."

The little boy looked wildly from one to the other.

"I won't go back!" he cried desperately. "Yer can't make me!"

Then he twisted underneath Tom's arm and, still clutching Barney, he was gone.

"He's got Barney!" cried Tom, chasing after the boy. "Come back, you little beggar!"

Emily hesitated. How could they catch the boy in the dark? And what if he fell and dropped Barney? She tried to think. The boy was the ghost, he must be. Perhaps he crept out of the hold at night to steal food – that must be how he'd been seen. So now, perhaps he would head for the entrance to the hold.

She blew out the candle. Captain Gray was always telling the passengers they must never use a naked light for fear of fire. Then she carefully retraced her steps to the entrance. She could hear bangs and thumps and curses as Tom crashed into the packing cases and casks. She just hoped the little boy knew the hold well enough not to trip and drop Barney, and that she was right, and he would try to get to the door.

The thumps were coming closer. She

crouched down in front of the door. There was a dim light beside it, and she knew if the boy saw her he would run away.

She heard running footsteps – soft, he couldn't be wearing shoes – and all of a sudden, there he was. She held her arms out, and he ran straight into them.

He gave up. His breath was coming in short, ragged gasps. Tom appeared, glaring at the boy, limping, and nursing his elbow.

"Where's Barney?" demanded Tom.

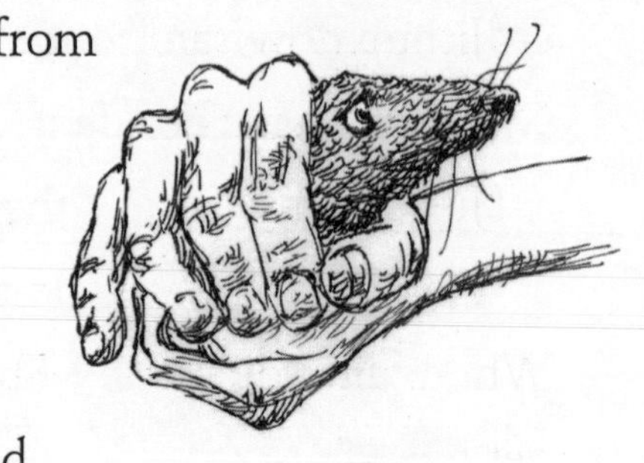

The boy looked from one to the other. Slowly, he held up his hands, which were clasped together. He opened his fingers a little, and through the gap appeared a little face with beady eyes. Barney was safe.

"Give him to Tom," said Emily gently. "Tom takes care of him."

"He didn't," retorted the boy. "He was going to leave him here, all by himself. But I would of looked after him."

"Cheeky little tyke," said Tom crossly, rubbing his elbow. "We were just hiding him to keep him safe."

"Like you," said Emily. "You were both hidden in the hold. What's your name?" she asked, still holding him so that he couldn't run away again.

"Jimmy," he said.

"Jimmy what?"

"Just Jimmy."

"And what are you doing here, Jimmy? Where did you come from? How did you get here?"

He looked up at her. His face was small and pointed, and his eyes looked too big for it. A bit like Barney, she thought.

"I ran away," he said. "From the workhouse. I hid under some sacks in a cart, and then I jumped off. An' I was near the docks, and I heard people talking, an' they said this ship was the greatest ship in the world, an' it was going to take 'em to a new country. An' I thought, well, that sounds better 'n Liverpool. So I found where the cargo was being loaded, an' when nobody was looking, I just nipped on. You won't tell, will yer? Only I'm not going back, I'm not!"

Emily tried to think. He couldn't stay here with the dark and the rats, she was quite sure of that. He was little more than skin and bones already. He needed someone to look after him.

And she knew just the person.

Tom went back to fetch Barney's hatbox, and the little procession set off for the captain's cabin, Emily with her arm firmly round Jimmy's shoulders in case he tried to run away. At the sight of the captain, tall and burly in his brass-buttoned uniform, Jimmy looked terrified, and shrank back. Emily's heart went out to him; he was so small, so thin, so frightened.

"It's all right, Jimmy. You're safe now, I promise. Would you like to hold Barney again?"

Jimmy gazed at her, his eyes wide and searching.

She took Barney out of the hatbox and put him gently into Jimmy's hands. "There. Stroke him. Just here, between his ears – he really likes that."

Captain Gray watched, his face a picture of bewilderment. "Two stowaways, a boy and a rat! And I have to say, the rat looks healthier than the boy. What has been going on aboard my ship? I've never seen such a thing, upon my word I haven't. You can tell me about the rat later. But this boy, where has he come from?"

"The hold," said Emily, "and before that, the workhouse." She told the captain what Jimmy had said, and by the time she had finished, Captain Gray was frowning angrily.

"It's a disgrace that children should be treated in such a way," he muttered, "in a great country like ours."

"I won't go back there," whispered Jimmy. "I'd rather jump in the sea."

The captain crouched down so that his face was level with Jimmy's.

"You shall not have to," he said seriously. "You have my word upon it. You are on the greatest ship in the world – my ship – and you're in my care now." He looked doubtfully at Barney. "As to the rat, I'm not sure whose care he's in!"

Thomas explained about Barney, and he and Emily looked anxiously at the captain.

"I see," he said. "Quite clearly, this is no ordinary rat." Then he looked at Jimmy, who still held Barney, stroking him gently. "For the time being, I think both hideaways can stay here."

Later, after a bowl of soup and a chunk of fresh bread, Jimmy curled up and went to sleep in the spare bunk in the captain's cabin. Emily tucked the blankets round him, and watched him for a moment. Then she turned to the others.

"Tell me about workhouses," she demanded. "What happens in them?"

The captain shook his head in disgust. "The poor who cannot support themselves are sent there. Men are separated from their wives, parents from their children. They are punished for being poor, not helped to rise above their state. They work long and terrible hours for food a pig would turn down. And the children... I've glimpsed them sometimes, through the gates. Their eyes are dead: they have no hope. Jimmy did well to escape. But thank heaven you found him when you did."

Emily tried to imagine such a place. Then another picture came into her head: a factory, a mill, where children choked on fibres of wool. Another place where children were not well treated. Would it be different in Australia? She didn't know what to think.

Suddenly, there was a commotion outside.

"I demand to see the captain!"

Emily's heart sank. She knew that voice. It was her father's.

"Ah, there you are, sir! My daughter, sir – she is missing, and I have reason to believe – ha! There he is!" He pointed a shaking finger at Tom. "I knew it, as soon as I heard she had been seen in the company of a steerage brat!"

The captain stood up, allowing Mr Ainsworth to see Emily. He spoke quietly, but with the authority of a man who knows he will be obeyed.

"Your daughter, sir, is a heroine. And Thomas Drew is a hero. Between them they have saved this child here from almost certain death – he is near to starvation. They are a credit to their parents, and to my ship. Let us have no more talk of brats, sir. It is not worthy of you."

Mr Ainsworth frowned. "I find this very difficult to believe."

"But believe it you must," said the captain. "And if you and your wife will graciously consent to dine at my table this evening, I shall have the very great pleasure of telling you all about what they have done."

"Not all, sir, I hope," said Emily after her father had gone, looking anxiously in the direction of Barney's hatbox.

The captain winked. "Indeed, no. I shall tell him only as much as he can cope with. Barney will be safe with me, but his care shall be in your hands. I draw the line at taking care of a rat, as well as a small stowaway and the greatest ship in the world!"

* * *

That night, Emily and Tom crept out on deck while their parents dined with the captain. The sky was navy blue and scattered with stars.

"I can't wait to be in Australia," said Tom, leaning on the railing and gazing at the silver pathway the moon made across the sea. "It's going to be wonderful. Everything will be different there."

Emily glanced at him.

"I don't really know much about Australia," she said. "You'll have to tell me."

He grinned. "Well, we've got plenty of time. Weeks and weeks and weeks..."

Emily smiled. What other surprises would her journey bring?

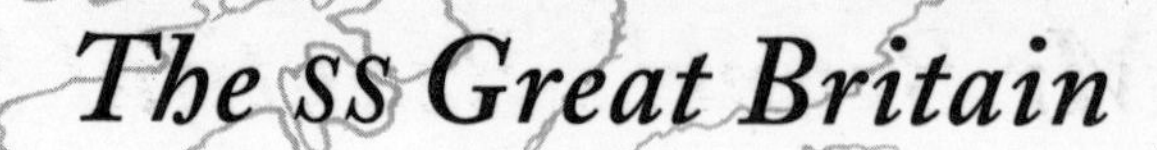

The *ss Great Britain*

On her maiden voyage across the Atlantic to New York, the *ss Great Britain* broke the previous speed record.

The *ss Great Britain* sailed around the world 32 times – more than 1,000,000 miles at sea.

In 1852, she made her first voyage to Australia, carrying 630 passengers. Hundreds of thousands of Australians are descended from emigrants who arrived on the *ss Great Britain*.

When the *ss Great Britain* was built in 1843, she was the biggest ship in the world, and the first ever iron-hulled, steam-powered passenger liner.

Built in Bristol, she was launched in the presence of Prince Albert. All the shops in the city were shut that day, and everyone turned out to cheer and wave flags. In Bristol Zoo Gardens, there was a fantastic firework display, with a firework picture of the ship surrounded by blazing sparkler fountains.

Mr Brunel's Beautiful Ship

The *SS Great Britain* was designed by the famous Victorian engineer Isambard Kingdom Brunel, who was also the chief engineer for the Great Western Railway, affectionately known as "God's Wonderful Railway".

The journey to Australia took 60 days. Passengers had to take their food with them. On one voyage, in 1864, the ship set out with 150 sheep, 30 pigs, 500 chickens, 400 ducks, 100 geese and 50 turkeys!

The ship was in use until 1933, when she was scuttled (allowed to sink) in a shallow bay in the Falkland Isles. Then, in 1970, she was brought back 8,000 miles to her birthplace in Bristol. Crowds of people lined the Avon Gorge to welcome her home, just as they had turned out for her launch. Since then, she has been beautifully restored. When you step on board, it's easy to imagine how it must have been for passengers like Emily and Tom.

Sue Purkiss

The first time Sue saw the *ss Great Britain* it was a shell: beautiful but empty. Not any more; now it's just as it was in its prime. You can peer into the cabins, wander through steerage and venture into the hold. It's full of memories; full of stories. She's so glad she was able to add one more!

James de la Rue

James grew up on the island of Guernsey and gets seasick, so it's just as well he likes flying. He loved visiting the *ss Great Britain* for the purposes of this book and was disappointed he had to leave after three hours – or was it four? Not surprisingly, he was glad that the ship wasn't moving up and down, despite the gales.

He now lives in Nottinghamshire with his wife and daughter.